Volpino, Last of the Chicken Thieves

Loris Malaguzzi set this tale in his native city of Reggio Emilia, located in the Po Valley in Italy. The tower, the square, the church, and the museum of natural history are all real parts of that city's historic core. This translation required much cooperation within the tightest constraints of time. Louise Cadwell produced a first version at top speed. In preparing its revision, I had the assistance of Lester Little.

Lella Gandini

ISBN 88-86277-44-X

© 1995 Edizioni Junior srl
24123 Bergamo, Via Pescaria 32

1 2 3 4 5 6 7 8 9 10
1995 1996 1997 1998 1999

Questo volume è stato stampato presso Cosmograf, Pedrengo (BG)

Finito di stampare nel mese di febbraio 1995

Loris Malaguzzi

Volpino, Last of the Chicken Thieves

Illustrations by Marie Horachova
Translated by Louise Cadwell and Lella Gandini

Edizioni Junior

This story begins
on the first night of spring.

A marvellous night
that gives
colored dreams to children,
soaring flights to little birds,
silver to the moon,
fragrance to the grass
and the walls.

It is such a special night,
that it even awakens from their long sleep
the thousand stuffed animals
in the museum of natural history:
including *Volpino*
the most clever and most famous
night hunter of chickens
who, captured and stuffed,
was put on view
fifty years ago or more.

"Volpino"
– the little birds call, –
*"why don't you come out with us
to look for the sun?
Grab onto this willow branch
and hold on tight".*

And so it happened that *Volpino*,
dressed up like Napoleon
(there is always one of Napoleon's coats
or hats in a museum),
escaped from the Lazzaro Spallanzani Museum
that first night of spring
with the help of a hundred little birds
and of the Great White Owl,
well-known for his sharp night vision
and his skill at playing the bassoon.

But this great night flight
did not last for long.
The little birds were not strong enough.
While for *Volpino*,
– with his fifty-year old hunger –
the craving to eat mounted.

Volpino, astronaut of the night,
disguised as Napoleon,
landed
– in full view of the roundest moon in the world –
on the tower of St. Prospero's Square:
the highest tower,
in the most beautiful square
at the stroke of midnight
on this first night of spring.
Meanwhile, the exhausted little birds
perched themselves
– to catch their breath –
on the cornice of the nearby church.

On the tower of St. Prospero
– the highest tower
in the most beautiful square –
Volpino remains alone.
Alone with the night,
the great moon,
the ravenous hunger,
his thoughts about food,
but also his old hunting instincts.

*"The chickens, the chickens,
they're near and they're fat!"*

And in fact,
down in the square,
a truck bearing chickens
arrives and stops,
to restock
the poultry shop.

The driver of the truck
– it is early, only four o'clock
in the morning –
pauses to nap.
For *Volpino*,
victory is at hand.

Old and invincible
chicken thief of the night
Volpino
climbs quickly down the tower
while the moon hides
behind a helpful,
passing cloud.

It's just like in the arena!

Volpino creeps along
stepping ever so lightly
with a sack in his paw.
A sack to fill up.

We're almost there!
Volpino is one step away
from the chickens.

But all of a sudden
Zap!…
a beam
like a brilliant spotlight
sent down by the moon
picks out *Volpino*.

"Watch out, Volpino"
the moon seems to say.

And the frightened *Volpino* steps back,
while the square
returns quietly to darkness.

Who can doubt
the courage of *Volpino*?

Volpino tries again
this time with lighter steps
and even greater determination.
We're almost there!
One step away from the chickens
his paw reaching out
But, all of a sudden
Zap!…
the beam of light
even brighter than before
– sent down by the moon –
spies on Volpino.
*"Watch out, Volpino,
you failed chicken thief!"*

Volpino stops, frightened.
Never in his life
had he been so persecuted
by the moon.

Volpino
changes his tactics.
This time he goes on the attack
hiding behind his sack.

But, once again, inexorable,
Zap!…
the moon is there again.

*"Volpino, be gone,
the game is up.
There is no
longer any room
in this world
for a poor
chicken thief".*

Who can doubt
the sharp mind of *Volpino*?

When the moon is an enemy
You need an old remedy.

*PUT A GAG ON HER, COVER HER UP,
TURN OFF HER LIGHT.*

What does it take?
A very long ladder
a bundle of wits
no fear of heights
the courage of a lion,
and, let's not forget,
Napoleon's coat.

*"Now, here I am,
moon,
wicked moon.
Now I will blind you
I will turn off
your light;
I will cover you up,
with the hat
and the coat
of Napoleon"*.

But while fearless *Volpino* is
carrying out his mission:
ZAP! a great gust of wind
blows down the ladder.

What will you do now, *Volpino*,
strong and unrivaled
chicken thief of the night,
hero of another time,
to return to earth?

History has it that
the adventure of *Volpino*
finishes here,
just like this,
on the moon.

It was an unexpected fate
for a great artist
a nocturnal chicken thief
an astronaut
without a license
and without glory.

Volpino has waited there now
for two hundred years
for someone
to come get him down…

So, children,
When you look up into the night sky,
Don't look only at the stars.
Look at the moon
and search for *Volpino*.

Volpino is there,
with his arms stretched out forever,
wearing Napoleon's coat.
And now you will understand that
Volpino's story is written in those shapes
that you see on the moon.

AND IT IS FOR THIS REASON
THAT WHEN NIGHT COMES
AND THE YELLOW MOON IS FULL
AND ALL HER DARK SHAPES APPEAR
THE DOGS
BARK AND BAY
WITH THEIR NOSES POINTING SKYWARD
IN PART OUT OF FEAR
IN PART BY PROFESSION
AND IN PART TO RECALL
THE STORY OF *VOLPINO*,
THE LAST, THE VERY LAST
OF THE CHICKEN THIEVES.